For Geoff and Savannah with love.

Table of Contents

Valentine's Day

"Marble" Painted Valentines 1
Valentine Clay Heart Mobile 2
Beaded Heart Napkin Rings. 3
Sweetheart Candy Frame. 4
Valentine Hearts Flowerpot 5
Valentine Clay Heart Trivet 7

St. Patrick's Day

Clover Painted T-Shirt 8
Lucky Clover Mobile 9
Clover Windsock 10

Easter

Starry Easter Eggs. 11
Diorama Egg 12
Easter Tree. 14
Jelly Bean Carrots 16

Mother's Day

Mom's Rose Teacup 17
"Stained Glass" Candle 18
Fabric Decoupage Plate 19
Mother's Day Jewelry Pin. 21
Mom's Message Center. 22

Father's Day

Dad's Leather Pencil Cup. 23
Father's Day "Tie" Card 24
Special Dad's Plaque 25
Decoupage Frame 27

Fourth of July

July 4th Fabric Wreath 28
Stars and Stripes Stationery 30
Stars and Stripes Basket 31

Halloween

Decorated Pumpkin. 32
Halloween Monster Claws 33
Ghostly Lollipops. 34
Domino Mask. 35

60 COOL Holiday Crafts for Year-Round Fun

Nancy Jo King

Lunchbox Press • Southlake, TX

No part of this publication may be reproduced in whole or in part, or stored in a retrieval system, or transmitted in any form or by any means, electronic, mechanical, photocopying, recording, or otherwise, without written permission of the publisher. For information regarding permission, write to Lunchbox Press, 701 Greymoor Place, Southlake, TX 76092.

ISBN 0-9678285-3-8

Copyright © 2001 Nancy King

All rights reserved.
Published by Lunchbox Press, 701 Greymoor Place, Southlake, TX 76092.

Interior Illustrations by Nancy Jo King

Photography by Lynne McCready

Cover and interior design © TLC Graphics, www.TLCGraphics.com.

Edited by Roxanne Camron

Printed in the United States of America

First printing, September 2001
Second printing, June 2002

Table of Contents

Thanksgiving

Potato-Printed Leaf Napkins 36
Leaf Napkin Rings 38
Nature Placemats.................. 40
Mini Bean Wreath 41

Hanukkah

Star of David 42
Gold Coin Wreath 43
Tissue Paper Gift Wrap 44
Star of David Gift Wrap 46
Decorated Beeswax Candles......... 48
Clay Menorah.................... 50

Christmas

Glitter Ball Ornaments 51
Poinsettia Napkin Rings............ 53
Peppermint Stick Vase............. 55
Candy Christmas Tree 56
Beaded Wreath Pin 57
Wreath of Hands 58
Candy Cane Reindeer.............. 60

Pinecone Christmas Tree........... 61
Cinnamon Stick Candle............. 62
Clay Ornaments................... 63
Punched-Tin Candleholder 64
Gold Pasta Wreath 65
Beaded Fruit 67
Paper Cone Ornament 68
Tissue Paper Trees 70

Kwanzaa

Woven Placemat................... 72
Beaded Candles 74

New Year's Eve

Party Hat 76
Confetti Placemats................. 78
Party Favors...................... 79
Treasure Box 80

Make Your Own Clay 83

v

Introduction

Want to really celebrate the holidays? Then get crafty with these 60 easy (we promise!) holiday crafts. No matter what the season, you'll find fun ideas for turning ordinary objects into works of art that you can give as gifts or keep for yourself. This year-round guide gives you step-by-simple-step instructions for making things like jewelry, stationery, candles, cards, and more!

Why Get Crafty?

One of the best ways to express yourself is through art. It gives you a chance to flex your creative muscles, explore your artistic talent, and put your mind to work on something other than schoolwork! As an extra bonus, you wind up with a really cool work of art that you made yourself. Besides, arts and crafts are just plain fun.

Getting the Gear

All of the materials needed to make the crafts in this book can be found at crafts or hobby stores; you might even have some of them at home already. If you can't find something, ask a sales associate to help you find the item or suggest a replacement.

VALENTINE'S DAY

"Marble" Painted Valentines

Stuff You Need

- three marbles
- three small paper cups
- three plastic spoons
- three colors of paint (red, pink, white)
- scissors
- 9- by 12-inch box (bottom or lid of a shirt box works great)
- several sheets of pastel construction paper
- plain cards or cardstock paper to make your own
- glue stick
- pen
- newspaper to cover work area

Impress your valentine with these fun to make cards!

What You Do

Put a small amount of paint in the paper cups — a different color in each one. Drop a marble in each cup.

Place a piece of pastel-colored construction paper in the bottom of the box. Trim, if necessary, so that the paper lies flat.

Pick up one of the marbles with a plastic spoon and place it onto the paper. Roll it around in the box so that it makes a swirling, abstract pattern. Repeat with the remaining colors. Let dry.

Trace or draw a heart on the "marbled" paper. Cut out. Glue onto the front of the plain card (or, if making your own card, fold the cardstock paper in half). Write desired message on the card and decorate. Repeat and make additional cards.

... Or Try This

This technique can be used to make a variety of projects such as handmade wrapping paper. You can also make cards for other holidays or occasions. Simply select a design that matches your theme and cut out of the "marbled" paper. Then glue onto your cards.

VALENTINE'S DAY

Valentine Clay Heart Mobile

Stuff You Need

- self-drying clay (colored modeling clays work great)
- heart-shaped mini cookie cutter
- rolling pin
- plastic knife
- toothpick
- waxed string (dental floss works great)
- ribbon for hanger
- small paintbrush (or nail)
- wax paper to cover work surface

You can use this clay technique to create mobiles with any holiday theme. Cookie cutters are great to use and come in tons of fun designs.

What You Do

Put a lump of clay on a hard surface work area. Roll out about three 4-inch balls of clay into slabs to make all of your hearts. Working from the center outward, use the rolling pin to roll out the clay. Use an even amount of pressure on the rolling pin to ensure your slab is uniformly 1/4 inch thick.

Use the mini cookie cutter to cut out the heart shapes. You'll want to make 20 hearts.

Use the end of a small paintbrush (or nail) to pierce a hole near the top and bottom of 15 of the hearts. Pierce a hole in the top part only of the remaining hearts. You'll use these holes to connect the hearts together as shown.

Roll out another slab of clay and draw one large heart using a toothpick. Cut out with the plastic knife. Use the end of the paintbrush (or nail) again and make one hole at the top of the heart and one hole near the bottom point of the heart. Make two more holes on each side near the bottom curve. Let all pieces dry completely.

To assemble the mobile, cut the waxed string into five 15-inch lengths. Thread four small hearts onto each string at each hole and tie a knot at each point to prevent hearts from sliding. Tie each string onto one of the holes at the bottom of the large heart and knot securely. Add a looped piece of ribbon to the hole at the top of the large heart and tie ends together forming a hanger.

Note: You can also make your own clay. See recipes on page 83.

VALENTINE'S DAY

Beaded Heart Napkin Rings

Stuff You Need

- thin-gauge copper or craft wire (thinner is easier to work with)
- needle-nose pliers
- cardboard tube from empty paper towel or bathroom tissue roll
- assorted beads
- heart-shaped beads
- (optional: old necklace or other jewelry beads)

Create bejeweled napkin holders and make a cool valentine craft using this jewelry-making technique.

What You Do

Wrap an 18-inch length of copper or other craft wire around the paper towel (or bathroom tissue) tube. The wire will go around a few times.

Use the needle nose pliers to form a small closed loop at one end.

Slip the wire off and begin threading the beads onto the straight end of the wire, sliding them onto the wire. Think about what pattern you want to create. You may do this with one color or style of bead or you can alternate color and style. Add the heart-shaped beads, one near each end, and one or more near the center of each wire coil.

When the wire is fully beaded, form another small closed loop at the other end to secure. Slide onto your rolled napkin.

... Or Try This

You can make this craft for any holiday or occasion. Simply coordinate your bead colors to match your theme — maybe red and green for Christmas, orange and black for Halloween, or pastels for Easter.

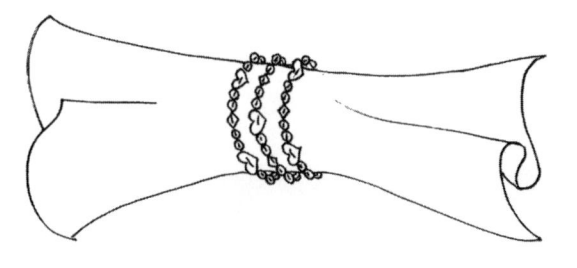

VALENTINE'S DAY

Sweetheart Candy Frame

Stuff You Need

- unpainted picture frame (may be wood or cardboard — available in craft stores)
- acrylic paint
- paintbrush
- "conversation hearts" candy
- white glue
- newspaper to cover work area

For Valentine's Day, show someone special just how much you care. Make this cute frame and put a picture of the two of you inside of it.

What You Do

Paint the frame in desired acrylic paint color — preferably a pastel to match your hearts. Let dry.

Glue on the conversation hearts candy all around the frame, overlapping them slightly. If desired, you can add a second layer of candy hearts.

... Or Try This

This same idea can be used for any holiday, theme, or occasion. For example, try round peppermint candies for Christmas, gold foil-wrapped coins for Hanukkah or candy corn for Halloween.

VALENTINE'S DAY

Valentine Hearts Flowerpot

Stuff You Need

- 6-inch clay terra-cotta flower pot
- white contact paper
- scissors
- pencil
- acrylic paint in four colors (one base coat and three coordinating colors)
- enough ribbon to go around pot and tie as shown
- sponge
- three paper plates
- newspaper to cover your work area

This project makes a fancy flowerpot to keep or give away. You can probably think of lots more creative uses for your decorated pot too. How about to hold all of your valentines?

What You Do

Begin by painting a base coat of paint onto the pot, below the rim. Let dry.

Trace and cut out heart shapes from the contact paper. For a size 6-inch clay pot, you will want to make about 12 cut-out stencils.

Remove the paper backing from each contact paper stencil and apply them to the clay pot, pressing down firmly to seal the edges. Place the stencils in any pattern you like, either random or symmetrical.

(continued on the next page)

Valentine Hearts Flowerpot (cont.)

Pour a little of your darkest color paint onto a paper plate. Cut into the sponge about an inch on the long side to form a handle to hold onto. Then use the rest of the sponge to dab the paint on with.

Dip the sponge into the paint, blot once on the paper plate, then press onto your pot, wherever you want to put that color. Press the sponge several times before you dip it in more paint.

Repeat with your other colors, letting the colors overlap. Let dry completely.

Remove the contact paper stencils. Tie the ribbon around your pot.

... Or Try This

Stenciling is great for more than just decorating flowerpots. How about a lampshade for your room? Match your décor by making a stencil that fits with your room's theme, match the colors, and you're all set. You can also make fantastic stationery and wrapping paper, or you can stencil and paint a border for your room.

VALENTINE'S DAY

Valentine Clay Heart Trivet

Stuff You Need

- self-drying clay (colored modeling clay works great)
- one sheet white paper
- pencil
- 10-inch piece of ribbon
- a straw
- wax paper to cover work area

This project makes a perfect gift for someone special on Valentine's Day.

What You Do

Trace or draw a heart of the desired size for your trivet on the white paper.

Pinch off several pieces of clay forming each into a 2-inch ball. You can make small coils by rolling them between your hands. To make larger coils, which are better suited to this project, roll the clay on a table. Use the palms of your hands and roll with even pressure. Begin rolling from the center of the clay and gradually move outward. This will help keep your coils even and uniform in thickness.

To form your base, make a long coil and shape it over the design you have drawn on the white paper. You may need several coils to go around the shape, so just overlap and press the edges together to connect the coils.

Roll six more coils from additional balls of clay. You will now alternate vertical and horizontal coils on top of the base, which will form a woven pattern. Trim or pinch off any excess.

Press the ends of each coil into the base coil to secure.

Use a straw to poke a hole into the top of your center vertical coil if desired. Later, you can loop your ribbon through.

Let clay dry thoroughly.

Note: You can also make your own clay. See recipes on page 83.

ST. PATRICK'S DAY

Clover Painted T-Shirt

Stuff You Need

- plain white T-shirt
- paper plate
- household sponge
- marker
- scissors
- green tempera or acrylic paint (or fabric paint)
- cardboard cut to fit inside T-shirt
- newspaper to cover work area

You can have the luck of the Irish with this clever clover design that's texture-painted with a sponge.

What You Do

Use the pattern shown here, or create your own clover design. Use the marker to draw the clover on the sponge. Cut out.

Place the cardboard inside the T-shirt to prevent the paint from bleeding through to the other side and to create a flat painting surface.

Put a small amount of green paint on a paper plate. Dip the sponge in the paint and blot once on the plate. Gently press the sponge paint-side down onto the T-shirt where desired. Repeat as often as you like. Try using different shades of green. You can make a lighter tint by adding white paint. Make a darker shade by adding black or dark blue paint.

Let dry thoroughly before handling.

... Or Try This

Sponge painting can be used for any holiday. Simply create your sponge motif or design to fit the occasion.

ST. PATRICK'S DAY

Lucky Clover Mobile

Stuff You Need

- one 9- by 12-inch sheet of green craft foam
- pen
- scissors
- round hoop (such as an embroidery hoop found in fabric stores)
- 1 1/2 yards of string
- cardstock or heavy paper
- (optional: Twisteez craft wire and needle-nose pliers)

Craft foam makes this project lots of fun! Look for it in fabric or crafts stores.

What You Do

Draw or trace a clover on heavy paper to create a stencil. It's easy if you think of a clover as three heart shapes, all connected at the points, and then just add a stem (or trace the pattern used for the sponge-painted T-shirt). Cut out.

Use this pattern to draw six (or more if desired) clovers on the craft foam. Cut each one out.

Use the pointed end of the pen to make a small hole at the top of each clover.

Cut the string into six different lengths ranging from 6 inches to 12 inches. Tie these around the hoop, evenly spaced apart. (Optional: If desired, instead of using string, use Twisteez craft wire. Cut your lengths a bit longer so you have some extra room to curl and twist the wire into loops before attaching your clovers to the ends. Twisteez craft wire is very pliable and easy to manipulate with the needle-nose pliers.)

Tie each clover onto the other end of the string. Cut another 12-inch piece of string and loop it to the top to serve as a hanger.

... Or Try This

Hang your mobile from a tree limb, on a hook from the ceiling in your room, on a curtain rod, or from a cup hook under a shelf.

ST. PATRICK'S DAY

Clover Windsock

Stuff You Need

- construction paper in white and different shades of green
- glue
- stapler
- scissors
- green crepe paper streamers
- pencil
- markers
- 12-inch piece of ribbon or string

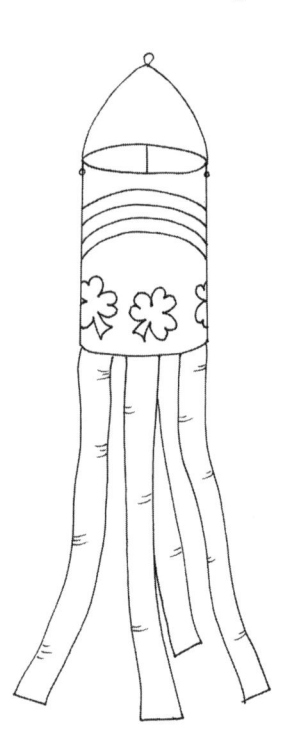

This fun craft will brighten up any room! You can make one for all kinds of occasions or use it as a party decoration.

What You Do

Start with one piece of white construction paper 9 inches by 12 inches. Keep it flat and place it horizontally so the long side is at the bottom.

Trace or draw some clovers on the green construction paper and cut them out. Glue these all over the white paper.

Use the markers to draw additional designs (such as rainbows, leprechauns, etc.) on the white paper.

Bring the shorter edges of the sides together forming a cylinder and glue (you might want to add a few staples at the top and bottom of the seam to secure).

Cut the green crepe paper streamers into four 18-inch lengths. Glue or staple each around the bottom edge of the windsock.

Using your pencil, poke two small holes in the sides of the top of the windsock and tie on the 12-inch string to be used as your hanger. Your windsock is ready to fly high.

...Or Try This

Windsocks make great party decorations. Make one for each guest. Personalize with their names, hang for the party and then give to your guests as a party favor!

EASTER

Starry Easter Eggs

Stuff You Need

- hard-boiled eggs, cooked and cooled
- oil pastel crayons
- star stickers
- plastic cups
- plastic spoons
- food coloring, white vinegar and water (or follow directions with commercial egg dye kit)
- newspaper to cover work area

These artistic Easter eggs will add pizzazz to your spring basket and are a snap to make.

What You Do

Press on the star stickers in a random pattern around your hard-boiled egg. Make sure edges are pressed down securely.

Using the oil pastel crayons, draw on swirling, curling lines around the stars. Think of "Van Gogh" colors like purple, green, yellow, white, and blue.

Fill a plastic cup with 1/2 cup water, add a few drops of desired food coloring and a teaspoon of white vinegar. Stir to mix. (Or follow directions for commercial egg dye.)

Gently drop the egg into the cup of dye. Let sit for a few minutes.

Remove with the plastic spoon and place in egg carton, or on paper towels to dry. Repeat as many times as you wish.

When completely dry, remove the star stickers.

EASTER

Diorama Egg

Stuff You Need

- white egg
- 6-inch piece of string
- small bead
- 8-inches of lace or decorative trim
- paint in pastel color
- small scissors
- glue
- paintbrush
- pencil
- small decoration (plastic or wooden bunny, figurine, or candy)
- cotton ball
- thin nail
- newspaper to cover work area

This age-old craft is always a favorite. Everyone, from young to old, can have fun making these special eggs.

What You Do

Draw an oval opening on the front of the egg. Carefully cut a hole in the front of the egg. Work slowly with small scissors to prevent cracking the shell. Little manicure scissors are perfect for this.

Empty out the egg (save it in an airtight container to cook or use in baking) and wash and thoroughly dry the eggshell.

Paint the shell of the egg as desired in a soft, pastel color. Let dry.

(continued on the next page)

12

Diorama Egg (cont.)

Put a small amount of white glue inside the base of the egg. Put the cotton ball on the glue and then add another drop of glue and gently place the small decoration (or candy) inside the egg. Hold in place until set (or place the egg back in an egg carton holder to keep it upright while it dries).

Carefully poke a small hole in the top of the eggshell using a thin nail. Loop the string and pass it through the hole. Thread the bead onto the ends (inside the egg). Knot the thread. The bead will prevent the string from pulling out when the egg is hung.

Add lace or trim around the edges of the opening, gluing in place. Trim off excess.

Easter Tree

Stuff You Need

- coffee can
- small square of florist's foam
- small tree branch
- white acrylic paint
- paintbrush
- construction paper in pastel colors
- scissors
- glue
- decorative moss
- decorations to hang
- newspaper to cover work area

Here's another fun project you can make with your whole family. Create your own decorations such as the Diorama Eggs or purchase little spring-themed ornaments.

What You Do

Find a tree branch with lots of little branches on it. Look for one that has already fallen off a tree. Paint the entire branch with the white acrylic paint and let dry.

Remove lid from the coffee can. Measure and cut one sheet of colored construction paper to fit around the can, overlapping edges. Glue on. Draw and cut out decorations from other colors of construction paper. (Optional: You may want to add lace or other decorative trim.)

(continued on the next page)

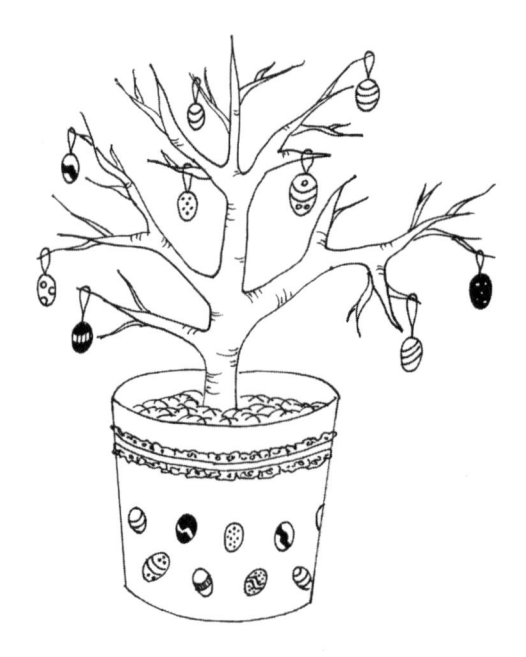

Easter Tree (cont.)

Cut and fit the florist's foam in the bottom of the can. Stick the painted branch down into the foam. Secure with a small amount of glue, if needed.

Cover the top of the foam with the decorative moss.

Hang your decorations from the branches and display!

... Or Try This

You can use this painted "tree" project for almost any holiday or occasion. Make and hang hearts for Valentine's Day. How about some scary Halloween decorations hanging on a painted-black tree branch? Or try a "Gumdrop Tree" for the Christmas holidays with gumdrop candies secured to the tips of each branch!

EASTER

Jelly Bean Carrots

Stuff You Need

- red, yellow, and green cellophane or plastic wrap
- marker
- clear tape
- scissors
- 8-inch piece of green curling ribbon (or raffia)
- one cup orange jelly beans

This project makes a super-cute party favor or extra special treat to add to any Easter basket.

What You Do

Cut one sheet each of the red and yellow cellophane to measure 12 inches. Place the yellow on top of the red. Draw a half circle that fills the size of cellophane. You can use a bowl, a plate, or any other round shape that's the right size as a guide. Cut out.

To make the cone-shaped carrot, find the half-way point of the 12-inch straight edge. Bring the two edges up together and overlap, forming a cone. Keep overlapping until you have a size "carrot" you like, keeping your point at the bottom. Tape securely (or, if using plastic wrap, it will self-adhere).

Fill with orange jellybeans, leaving enough room at the top to gather and twist closed.

Cut a 6- by 4-inch strip of the green cellophane. Wrap this around the top of the gathered orange ends. Tie tightly with the ribbon or raffia. Curl the ends of the ribbon with the scissors.

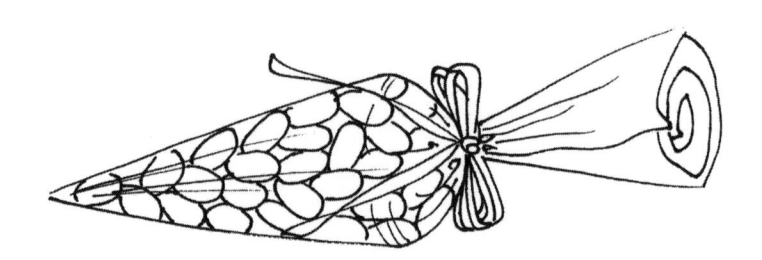

Mom's Rose Teacup

Stuff You Need

- china cup and saucer (look in thrift or antique shops)
- florist's foam (small block to fit inside teacup)
- moss (available in florist or craft shop)
- approximately 12 to 15 dried roses (with stems attached)
- needle-nosed pliers
- scissors

Let Mom or a special grandmother know how much you love her with this delicate rose teacup!

What You Do

Cut the florist's foam to fit inside the teacup. Press it down into the cup.

Cover the top of the foam with the moss.

Cut each rose so that about 1 1/2 - 2 inches of stem remain. Press the stem gently through the moss and into the foam in the teacup. It may be helpful to use the needle-nosed pliers to hold the stem, just under the flower. Then push it into the foam without damaging the dried flower. Repeat with the remaining roses.

Place the teacup in the saucer and it's ready to present to your favorite mom.

MOTHER'S DAY

"Stained Glass" Candle

Stuff You Need

- candle in a clear glass container
- tissue paper in a variety of colors
- decoupage glue
- paintbrush
- three pieces of thin ribbon cut into 12-inch lengths
- scissors
- newspaper to cover your work area

Adult supervision required

Both mom and grandmom will light up when you make this unique candle holder. When a candle's burning, the soft colors of the tissue paper reflect beautifully.

What You Do

Tear or cut the tissue paper in a variety of colors into 1-inch square pieces.

Using the brush, paint the decoupage glue onto the outside of the glass container. Work in small sections.

Place of piece of tissue paper on the glue. Brush more glue on top.

Continue applying the tissue paper, slightly overlapping each piece, until the entire outside of the container is covered. Let dry.

Tie the three pieces of ribbon around the top rim of the container. Make a pretty bow and trim the edges.

... Or Try This

Create a centerpiece or table display by making several candleholders to group together. Try using jars of different heights.

Careful! Always use adult supervision when lighting candles!

MOTHER'S DAY

Fabric Decoupage Plate

Stuff You Need

- one clear glass plate (any size)
- color-coordinated fabric scraps
- decoupage glue
- paintbrush
- scissors
- newspaper to cover work area

What You Do

Cut your fabric scraps in small pieces, approximately 2-inches square. The number of squares you need will depend on what size plate you are using.

Lay your plate facedown on the newspaper. Working in small sections, brush on the decoupage glue to the back of the plate. Place one of the fabric pieces right side down over the glue, arranging it so that it comes just to the edge of the plate, but does not hang over. Brush more of the decoupage glue over the fabric, working from the center of the piece of fabric outwards, gently pressing out any air bubbles.

Continue to arrange the fabric in this method, slightly overlapping pieces, until the entire back of the plate is covered.

(continued on the next page)

Fabric Decoupage Plate (cont.)

Let dry. This may take overnight.

Note: Decoupage won't hold up to repeated washing, so use the plate as a decorative item!

...Or Try This

You can also make this craft using clear plastic plates. In place of fabric, you can use decorative-patterned origami papers or thick wrapping paper.

MOTHER'S DAY

Mother's Day Jewelry Pin

Stuff You Need

- watercolor paper (thicker works better — try to find 140 lb. weight)
- watercolors
- paper cup
- water
- paintbrush
- pin-backing
- clear nail polish
- glue
- sequins
- rhinestones

Each of these pins is a one-of-a-kind work of art. They're as much fun to make as they are to wear!

What You Do

Tear an oval shape about 2 inches wide out of the watercolor paper. Tearing gives a nice soft edge to the pin.

Brush water all over the torn paper. Dip your brush in the water, twirl it in one color of paint, apply it to the wet paper, and watch the color bleed. Repeat with other colors as desired. Let dry.

Lay the dried paper under something heavy (like a stack of books) overnight to flatten it out.

Paint a coat of clear nail polish over the surface. Glue sequins and/or rhinestones to the jewelry to make it even more sparkly.

Glue the pin backing to the reverse side of the pin.

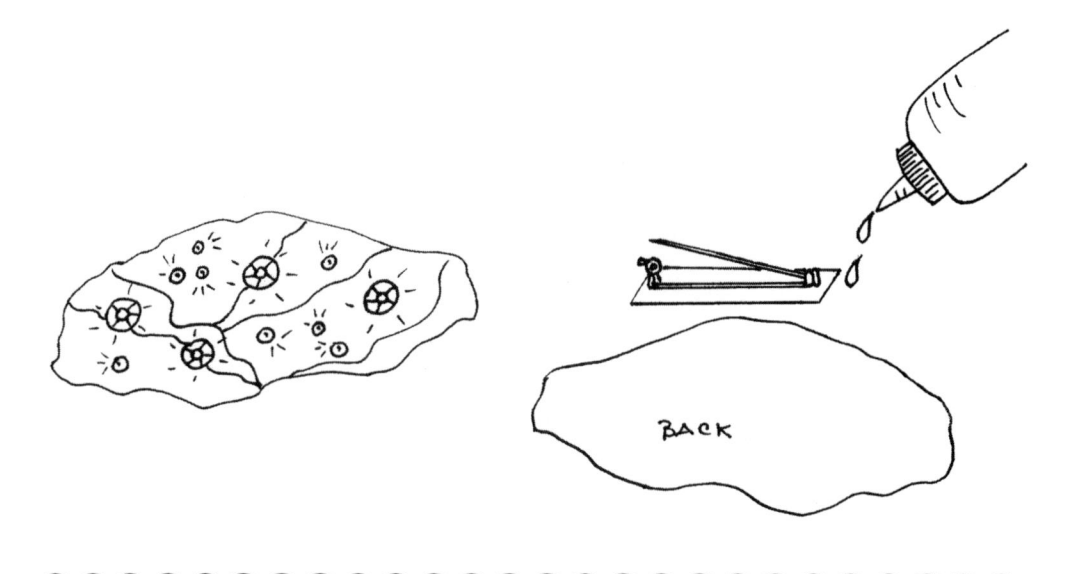

MOTHER'S DAY

Mom's Message Center

Stuff You Need

- 12- by 12-inch piece of cork tile or old bulletin board
- green felt
- scissors
- felt in assorted colors
- pencil
- push-pins
- glue stick and white glue
- picture hanger, if needed

Leave special photographs and love notes on this cheerful springtime message center you make yourself.

What You Do

Measure and cut the green felt to fit the corkboard. Glue it down using the glue stick. Press firmly from the center outwards, smoothing out to avoid getting air bubbles.

Cut out flower designs you've drawn or traced onto the colored felt. Decorate the corkboard by gluing (use the white glue for this) flowers around the edges. Use as few or as many flowers as you like!

If needed, attach a hanger to the corkboard or bulletin board.

Make smaller flowers out of felt and glue onto the heads of push-pins.

. . . Or Try This

You can also make this craft using ribbon roses or silk flowers as decorative accents!

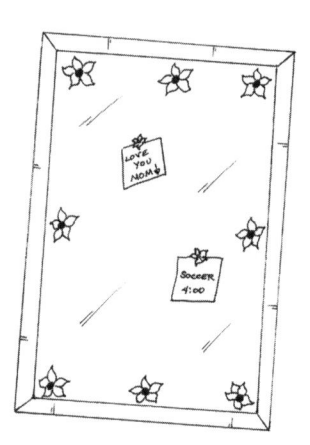

Dad's "Leather" Pencil Cup

Stuff You Need

- frozen juice can (with top lid removed)
- 1-inch wide masking tape
- brown shoe polish
- old rag or cloth
- newspaper to cover work area
- optional: rubber gloves to keep hands clean

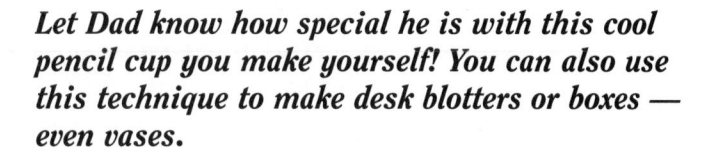

Let Dad know how special he is with this cool pencil cup you make yourself! You can also use this technique to make desk blotters or boxes — even vases.

What You Do

Tear the masking tape into small pieces, about 1-inch long. Stick onto the sides of the juice can. Press firmly by rubbing down on the tape. You should tear the masking tape rather than cutting it, as it is important to have a soft, leather-like edge. Cover the entire container.

Apply the brown shoe polish all over, using the applicator brush that comes with the polish.

Rub off the excess polish with an old piece of cloth or rag to give the aged look of leather.

... Or Try This

To make a desk blotter, purchase a plain blotter from the store. Cover the vinyl edges of the blotter as described above. You can also use old cigar-type boxes for cool containers. To make vases, use unusual shaped bottles.

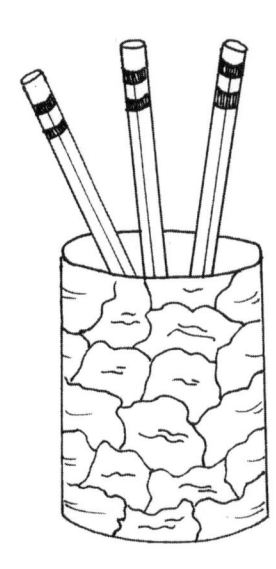

FATHER'S DAY

Father's Day "Tie" Card

Stuff You Need

- 12- by 18-inch piece of white construction paper
- markers
- scissors
- glue
- wallpaper scraps

A handmade card is always a special gift!

What You Do

Fold white construction paper in half.

In the center of the front cut a 2-inch slit down from the top of the card.

Fold down these corners to form a "shirt collar" as shown.

Cut a tie shape from the wallpaper. Glue it under the shirt collar down the center of the front of the card.

Use marker to write a message on the card.

... Or Try This

Maybe your dad or grandpa is more of a bow tie kind of guy, or you might experiment with a western theme. Use crayons to color a denim or plaid "flannel" background on your white paper. Instead of a tie, cut two pieces of shoelace string and glue them down under the collar. Cut out a lariat fastener (such as a horseshoe, star, horsehead, cactus, etc.) from the construction paper. Glue it over the lariat strings about halfway down, leaving the ends to hang.

FATHER'S DAY

Special Dad's Plaque

Stuff You Need

- 5-inch by 7-inch wood plaque or board
- sandpaper
- foil baking sheet with smooth bottom or heavy aluminum foil
- scissors
- hammer
- nails
- picture hanger
- pencil
- paper
- tape
- paint
- paintbrush
- paper plate
- newspaper to cover work area

Adult supervision required

Dad will love a gift you made yourself because it shows how much you care!

What You Do

If needed, sand the edges of your wooden board to make sure it's smooth.

Pour a small amount of paint onto the paper plate and use the brush to paint the top and sides of the wood. Paint the area that will be exposed after you attach your foil piece. Let dry.

Carefully cut the foil baking sheet or foil a little smaller than your wooden board.

Center the foil over the wooden plaque and hammer a small nail into each corner to secure.

Cut the piece of paper the same size as your foil. Draw a picture you know Dad will like on the paper. Keep your design simple, something like a heart, sailboat, star, etc. will work best! Tape the paper over the foil.

(continued on the next page)

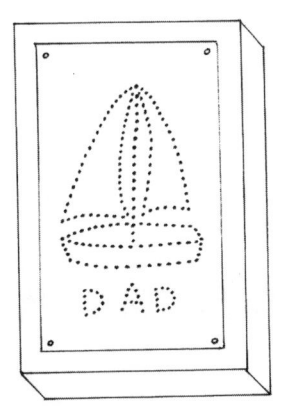

Special Dad's Plaque (cont.)

Use the hammer and nail to punch holes following the outline of the drawing. When complete, remove the paper and you will have transferred your design onto the foil! Add a picture hanger to the back.

... Or Try This

Make your own award plaques. This is a great craft idea when you want to acknowledge someone's achievements or to say thank you to someone special.

Careful! Ask an adult to help you hammer, handle the foil, and punch the holes.

FATHER'S DAY

Decoupage Frame

Stuff You Need

- unpainted picture frame about 1-inch wide
- decoupage glue
- wrapping paper
- paint — acrylic, craft, or tempera
- paintbrush
- scissors
- paper plate
- newspaper to cover work area

This gift will be even more special if you include a picture of you and your dad!

What You Do

Pour a small amount of paint onto the paper plate. Use the brush to paint the frame. Let dry.

Cut out pictures from the wrapping paper. Try to select a design you know your Dad will like such as golf, fishing or other sports, ducks or wildlife.

Working in small sections, brush a small amount of decoupage glue onto your frame. Press one of the cut-out pictures over the just-glued area. Brush on another layer of glue on the top of the picture, pressing out any air bubbles. Repeat as desired until as much of the frame is decorated as you like. Brush on one final coat of decoupage glue over the entire frame. Let dry.

Fill it with a drawing, a note, or a photograph.

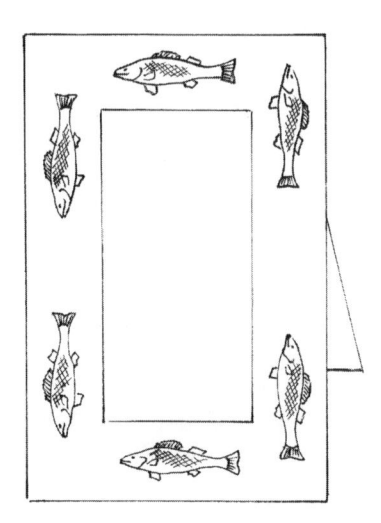

4TH OF JULY

July 4th Fabric Wreath

Stuff You Need

- small straw or raffia wreath (available at fabric and craft stores)
- pinking shears
- three small flags (on little poles)
- fabric: red, white, blue solids, and patriotic patterns
- pencil

This wreath is fun to make alone or with help from your family and friends. It looks really super, but is super-easy to put together!

What You Do

Use the pinking shears to cut out 3- by 3-inch squares of the assorted fabrics. (The quantity will depend on the size of wreath you have, but a 7 1/2-inch diameter wreath will use approximately 100 squares.) The pinking shears give a decorative finish to the fabric.

Hold a pencil pointed down towards the center of each square (fabric must be right-side up), and press it into the straw wreath. This will gather the fabric and cause it to flare out from the wreath.

(continued on the next page)

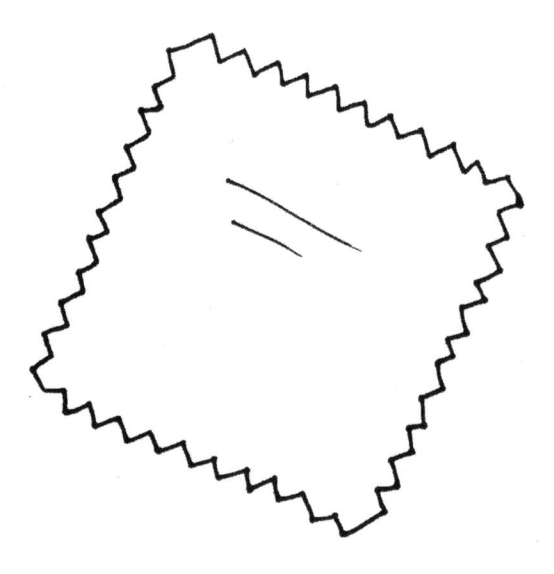

July 4th Fabric Wreath (cont.)

Repeat, alternating colors and designs, to form a pleasing pattern. Fill the entire top and sides of the wreath.

Finish by sticking the flags into the wreath.

...Or Try This

This project is a great technique that can be adapted for any holiday or occasion. Simply select coordinating fabrics and decorations!

4TH OF JULY

Stars and Stripes Stationery

Stuff You Need

- hole-punch
- plastic lid (disposable)
- white paper
- paper plate
- red and blue paint — acrylic, craft, or tempera
- flat stencil brush
- small-tipped paintbrush

Show your patriotic spirit on our country's birthday with this stars and stripes stationery.

What You Do

Trace or draw a star design on the plastic lid.

Use a hole-punch to punch out small holes following the outline of your star. This will be your stencil.

Lay the stencil flat over your white paper. If you want your stationery folded, like note-cards, fold it first so you will know where to place your stencil. If desired, use a small amount of masking tape to hold it in place while you work.

Put a small amount of the blue paint onto a paper plate. Using a stencil brush with a flat tip, dip the brush into the paint and blot once. Hold your brush at a 90-degree angle, right over your stencil. Press the brush down on the stencil and use small "dabbing" strokes so the paint goes in all of the exposed holes of the stencils. Let dry.

Remove the stencil. Use the red paint and the small-tipped brush to paint red stripes and accent lines around your stars. These lines can be straight or wavy. If desired, use a ruler to make straight lines.

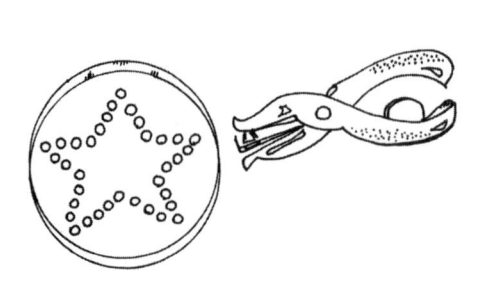

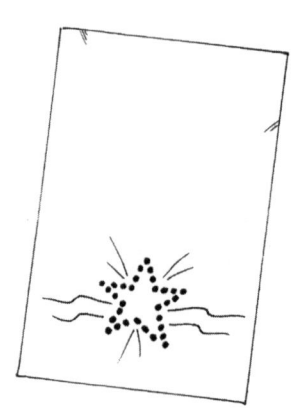

4TH OF JULY

Stars and Stripes Basket

Stuff You Need

- rectangular-shaped basket
- red, white, and blue paint — acrylic, craft, or tempera
- three paper plates
- star stickers
- paintbrush
- sponge
- scissors
- 1/2 yard ribbon
- newspaper to cover work area

This patriotic basket will be a real hit when you display it on a table as a decoration. You can also fill it with bright red and white flowers and tie on a blue bow!

What You Do

Mark off a square in the upper left corner of each long side of the basket. This square should be about one third the height of your basket and the same distance wide. Pour some white paint on a paper plate and use the brush to paint this square white. Let dry thoroughly.

Press star stickers onto the dried white square, arranging in rows. Put some blue paint on a paper plate. Dip the sponge in the blue paint, blot once on the paper plate, and then press the sponge onto the white square until the white square is covered with the blue paint.

When the blue paint is thoroughly dry, remove the star stickers to reveal the white star shapes.

Pour some red paint on a paper plate. Use the brush to paint red stripes on every other woven band of the basket. Pour some white paint on another paper plate. Paint the other stripes white. Let dry.

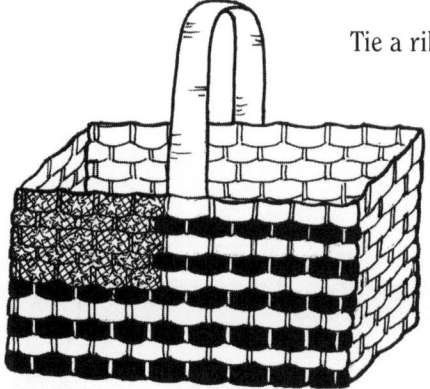

Tie a ribbon onto the basket handle.

HALLOWEEN

Decorated Pumpkin

Stuff You Need
- pumpkin
- straight pins
- pencil
- assorted beads
- assorted sequins

This Halloween, try something a little different than last year's carved jack-o-lantern. Dazzle your friends and family with this sparkling pumpkin.

What You Do

Begin by selecting a design and drawing it onto your pumpkin. Here are some suggestions:

- Write your name on the pumpkin
- Draw on a jack-o-lantern face
- Trace a heart, flower, stars, or other design
- Use your imagination to create a free-form design

Thread a bead, followed by a sequin, onto a straight pin. Try some interesting color schemes such as an orange bead with a black sequin.

Stick the beaded straight pins into the pumpkin, following the design lines you drew.

. . . Or Try This

Try adding rhinestones to create a glittering effect. Simply glue on inexpensive "crystal" rhinestones on your drawn design lines or in a random pattern.

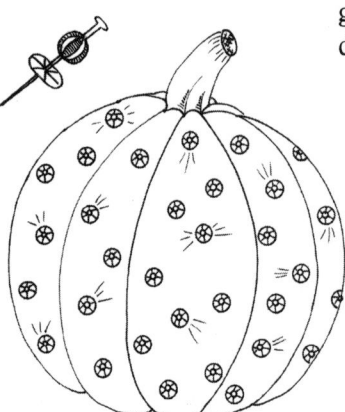

Halloween Monster Claws

Stuff You Need

- white gloves (found in hardware/gardening stores)
- glue
- fun fur (found in craft/fabric stores)
- black felt
- scissors
- permanent fabric markers

Add some scary Halloween fun to your trick or treating. These monster claws are sure to be a hit!

What You Do

Cut the fun fur to desired shapes, such as "tufts" of hair. Glue these onto the gloves.

Cut "fingernails" from the black felt. Glue on.

Use the permanent fabric markers to draw on scars, blood, veins, and all the scary things you can think of!

... Or Try This

Make your gloves like a tiger's paw with black felt stripes and claws and orange fake fur. Or get fancy by using white cotton dress gloves with red felt fingernails, and glue jewels on the fingers to be your jewelry.

HALLOWEEN

Ghostly Lollipops

Stuff You Need

- round, pre-wrapped lollipops
- white tissue paper
- orange ribbon (8-inches long)
- black marker
- scissors

Be the favorite house on the block when you pass out these delightful treats!

What You Do

Cut out several 8-inch squares of white tissue paper for each lollipop. Also cut one 8-inch long piece of orange ribbon for each.

Put the lollipop in the center of the stacked tissue and tie the ribbon around it to make the head and body.

Use the black marker to draw on a face. Have fun with your faces. Make different expressions on each one.

HALLOWEEN

Domino Mask

Stuff You Need

- one piece of white cardboard
- 10-inch piece of elastic
- pencil
- hole punch
- scissors
- markers
- sequins
- feathers
- rhinestones
- glue

Keep your identity a secret with this handmade mask. Let your next party be a true masquerade.

What You Do

Enlarge and use the pattern below to trace and cut one domino mask out of the white cardboard. Carefully cut out the eye shapes.

Use the marker to color and decorate your mask. Experiment with color themes and designs. Your mask can be abstract or represent something real, such as an animal or bird.

Glue on the rhinestones, sequins, and feathers.

Punch a hole in each side of the mask. Tie on the elastic string, adjusting to fit properly around your head.

... Or Try This

Attach your domino mask to a thin 12-inch wooden dowel, which will serve as a handle. This way you can carry your mask, and simply cover your eyes whenever you want to be mysterious!

THANKSGIVING

Potato-Printed Leaf Napkins

Stuff You Need

- light-colored cloth or paper napkin
- potato
- pencil
- plastic knife
- tempera or acrylic paint in several fall shades (gold, red, yellow)
- paper plate
- newspaper to cover work area

These lovely napkins will add a creative handmade touch to your Thanksgiving dinner! They can be made with cloth or paper napkins.

What You Do

Cut the potato in half and use the pencil to trace or draw a simple leaf design on it.

Use the plastic knife to cut around the design (about 1/4" deep).

Cut from the sides of the potato to the edge of the design to remove excess. This leaves the design "raised" for printing.

Pour a small amount of the different colors of paint close together on the paper plate.

(continued on the next page)

Potato-Printed Leaf Napkins (cont.)

Dip the potato stamper in the paint, swirling it a little in each color. Blot once, then press onto your napkin. Be sure not to move the stamper while you are printing to prevent smearing. Repeat design as desired. Let dry and enjoy!

... Or Try This

You can make so many things with this super-simple printing technique. Make cards, stationery, T-shirts, or print a design border on the walls of your room to match your décor!

THANKSGIVING

Leaf Napkin Rings

Stuff You Need

- scissors
- cardboard tube from empty paper towel or bathroom tissue roll
- pencil
- glue
- tempera or acrylic paint in several fall colors (gold, red, yellow)
- paintbrush
- paper plate
- leaf (real, silk, or construction paper)
- newspaper to cover work area

This craft is the perfect complement to your potato-printed leaf napkins. Or, change your motif and make napkin rings for any holiday or occasion!

What You Do

Measure and draw a line around the paper towel tube, approximately 1 1/2 inches from the end. Cut out one 1 1/2-inch section for each napkin ring.

Pour a small amount of the different colors of paint close together on the paper plate.

Dip the brush into the paint, swirling a little of each color onto the brush, and paint the outside and inside of the paper towel tube. Let dry completely.

(continued on the next page)

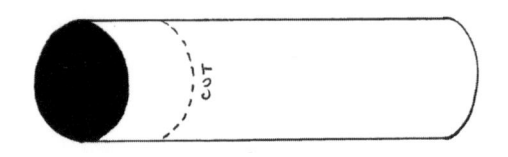

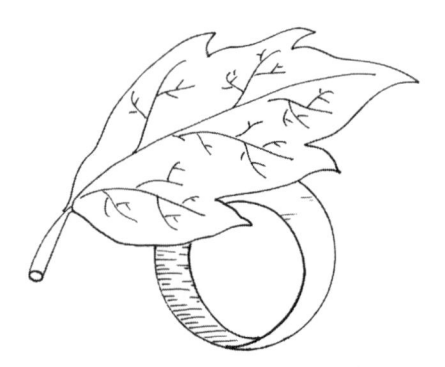

Leaf Napkin Rings (cont.)

Add a small amount of glue onto the back of the leaf and press onto the top of the paper towel tube so that the leaf lies flat when the napkin ring is positioned to hold a napkin. Let dry. Place a napkin inside and enjoy!

... Or Try This

Find a photograph of each of your guests. Cut out the pictures, glue on a little construction paper frame, and use this to glue onto your napkin ring. Or use dried or silk roses, seashells, buttons, or tiny treasures like old jewelry. Let your imagination go!

THANKSGIVING

Nature Placemats

Stuff You Need

- assorted leaves
- paper plate
- acrylic paints in fall colors (red, yellow, gold, orange)
- scissors
- paintbrush
- hole punch
- one yard felt-backed vinyl (or a purchased vinyl tablecloth)
- paper towel
- newspaper to cover work area

Set a festive autumn table with these easy-to-make placemats.

What You Do

Cut the vinyl into 12-inch by 18-inch rectangles for each placemat. Cut the two 12-inch side edges into a decorative curvy shape, like a scallop or free-form design. Use the hole-punch to make holes about an inch apart going around the border.

Place a small amount of each color of paint onto the same paper plate. Select a leaf, then brush paint on the entire top surface. Experiment with mixing the colors by dabbing on a little bit of each of them — one color on top of the other.

Turn the leaf over and press it paint-side down onto the vinyl placemat. Cover with a piece of paper towel and gently, taking care not to let it slide around, press with your hand. This will transfer the paint from the leaf onto the placemat, making a print.

Repeat with other leaves until you have a pleasing design. Let dry.

THANKSGIVING

Mini Bean Wreath

Stuff You Need

- assorted dried beans
- glue
- water
- plastic container lid (such as a lid from a margarine container)
- wax paper
- disposable bowl
- plastic spoon or craft stick
- 10-inch piece of raffia, twine, or other natural fiber ribbon

These mini-wreaths are so fun and easy to craft, you'll want to make more than one.

What You Do

In a plastic or paper disposable bowl, very slightly thin the glue (3 parts glue to 1 part water).

Mix in about 3/4 of a cup of beans and stir until all the beans are well coated with the glue.

Place a sheet of wax paper over the plastic lid, with the rim facing up.

Press the bean mixture onto the wax paper inside the lid. Use the plastic spoon or craft stick to make a circle in the center of the beans, forming a ring with the beans. Let dry thoroughly.

Tie on the raffia or twine and make a pretty bow.

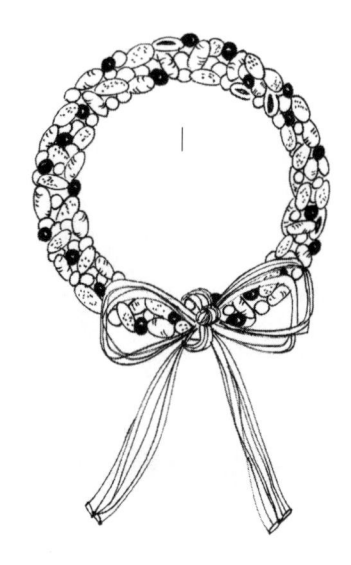

HANUKKAH

Star Of David

Stuff You Need

- six ice cream craft sticks
- glue
- silver paint — acrylic, craft, or tempera
- paintbrush
- silver glitter
- decorative cord for hanging
- newspaper to cover work area

Make several of these to hang in your window for a special Hanukkah display!

What You Do

Glue three sticks to form a triangle. Repeat with the other three sticks.

Fit the triangles together and glue edges as shown to form a six-pointed star.

Paint with the silver paint. While the paint is still wet, sprinkle with the silver glitter. Let dry.

Attach a cord to the top for hanging.

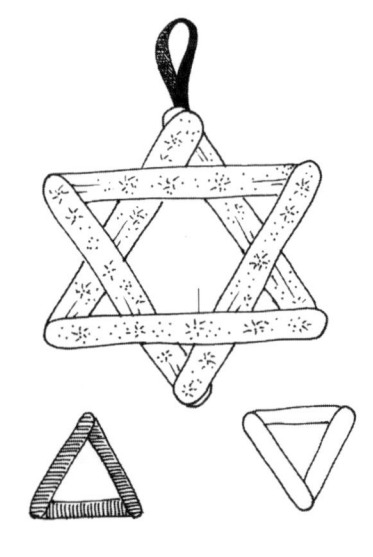

HANUKKAH

Gold Coin Wreath

Stuff You Need

- two paper plates
- pencil
- scissors
- silver paint
- paintbrush
- glue
- 12-inch piece of silver ribbon
- hole punch
- paper clip
- approximately 40 gold foil-covered chocolate coins
- bowl or other round-shaped item
- newspaper to cover work area

Here's a cool Hanukkah craft using symbolic gelt (chocolate coins) to celebrate the season!

What You Do

Use a bowl or other round shape to draw a circle about 6 inches across on a paper plate. Cut out.

Draw a smaller circle inside and cut this out to form a ring.

Use the hole punch and make two holes about one inch apart near the top of the ring. Open up the paper clip and form a ring shape. Loop it through the two holes to create a hanger.

Pour some silver paint onto a paper plate. Paint the front of the ring. Let dry.

Glue on the gold foil-covered chocolate coins. Overlap a second layer on top. Let dry.

Tie on the silver ribbon, and make a bow.

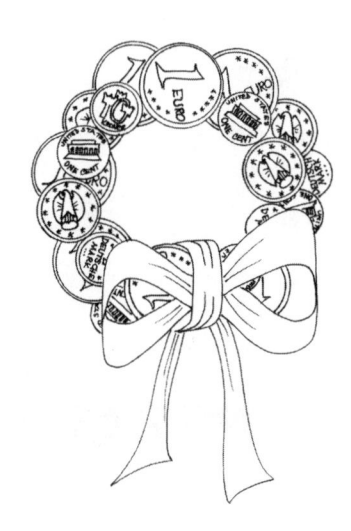

HANUKKAH

Tissue Paper Gift Wrap

Stuff You Need

- waxed paper (found in the grocery store)
- colored tissue paper (shades of blue)
- iron and ironing board
- newspaper to cover work area

Adult supervision required

Wrap up your Hanukkah gifts in make-it-yourself paper in shades of blue and white.

What You Do

Tear the tissue paper into small shapes or squares. Use several different shades of blue.

Place a piece of newspaper on the ironing board. Place one sheet of waxed paper (cut to desired size) on top of the newspaper. Carefully arrange the pieces of torn tissue paper on top of the waxed paper.

Cut a second piece of waxed paper the same size as the first. Gently place it on top of the tissue paper (take care not to scatter the tissue!).

(continued on the next page)

Tissue Paper Gift Wrap (cont.)

Place another piece of newspaper on top. With the iron on a low setting, run your iron over the newspaper. It will help to work from the center out to the edges. The heat will bond the two pieces of waxed paper together, sealing the tissue inside.

First, wrap your gift in a piece of white paper or tissue. Wrap it again with the waxed paper you have created with your tissue paper showing through. Match your ribbon to the color of tissue paper to really make this a standout.

Careful! Ask an adult to help you with the ironing step of this project.

HANUKKAH

Star of David Gift Wrap

Stuff You Need

- gold and silver paint — acrylic, craft, or tempura
- sponge
- scissors
- white butcher paper (sold on a roll)
- pencil
- paper plate
- tape
- newspaper to cover work area
- optional: silver glitter

This creative sponge-painting technique can be used to make more than gift wrap. Try it on note cards, stationery, or book covers!

What You Do

Roll out a section of white butcher paper. Working in sections about two feet long will work well. Tape the paper down on the corners to secure it to a tabletop covered in newspaper.

Draw a triangle on the sponge. Cut out.

Put a small amount of silver and gold paint on a paper plate. Dip the sponge in the paint, blot once on the paper plate, then press it gently onto the white paper. To avoid smudges, take care not to let the sponge move. You can press several times before you dip the sponge back into more paint.

(continued on the next page)

Star of David Gift Wrap (cont.)

Turn the sponge around so the points of the triangle face the opposite direction. Dip in paint and press over each triangle, creating the six-pointed Star of David.

Repeat as desired all over the paper. If desired, sprinkle on silver glitter to each star while the paint is wet. Let dry thoroughly.

... Or Try This

Glue a piece of thin silver or copper wire between two stars to add to the top of the gift as a decoration! Loop and twirl the wire before connecting it to the ribbon

HANUKKAH

Decorated Beeswax Candle

Stuff You Need

- two 8- by 16-inch sheets of beeswax (two different colors) and one 12-inch piece of wick (sold in craft stores)
- scissors
- plastic knife
- ruler

The eternal flame is one of the symbols of the Festival of Lights. These awesome beeswax candles are very fragrant and don't drip or smoke.

What You Do

The wick should be about 1 inch longer than the candle you want to make. For these 4-inch pillar candles, cut your wick into two 5-inch pieces.

Use your ruler to measure out a 4- by 16-inch piece of beeswax. (One sheet will make two 4-inch pillar candles). Using your plastic knife or scissors, cut out your wax piece.

The wick should be placed near the edge of the beeswax. The first roll is the most important as it needs to be very tight and even. Crimp the wax around the wick and pinch evenly until the entire edge is sealed. Roll tightly and evenly and then seal the end by smoothing the seam with pressure from your thumbs.

(continued on the next page)

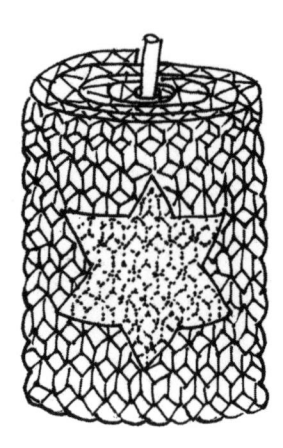

Decorated Beeswax Candle (cont.)

Use a different color of beeswax to cut out decorations. One of the great things about beeswax is that pieces will stick together because of the waxy texture. Simply cut out shapes and stick onto the sides of your pillar candle, pressing into the candle.

...Or Try This

You can make menorah candles with beeswax. Simply make eight candles the same size and make one taller. You can also decorate beeswax with sequins, rhinestones, shells, or beads! Let your imagination go wild!

Careful! Always ask for an adult's help when lighting a candle.

HANUKKAH

Clay Menorah

Stuff You Need

- homemade clay (see recipes on page 83)
- rolling pin
- five straws
- scissors
- yellow construction paper
- orange crayon or marker
- glue
- foam meat tray

Celebrate Hanukkah with this cool handmade menorah your whole family will enjoy.

What You Do

Make the clay by mixing ingredients in a large bowl and follow instructions for kneading.

Roll out the clay into an oblong shape and place on the top of the meat tray.

Cut four of the straws in half. Stick the long straw into the center of the clay. Place the four short straws on each side.

From the yellow construction paper, cut nine "flames." Color some orange fire in the center of each.

Glue a flame inside the top of each straw.

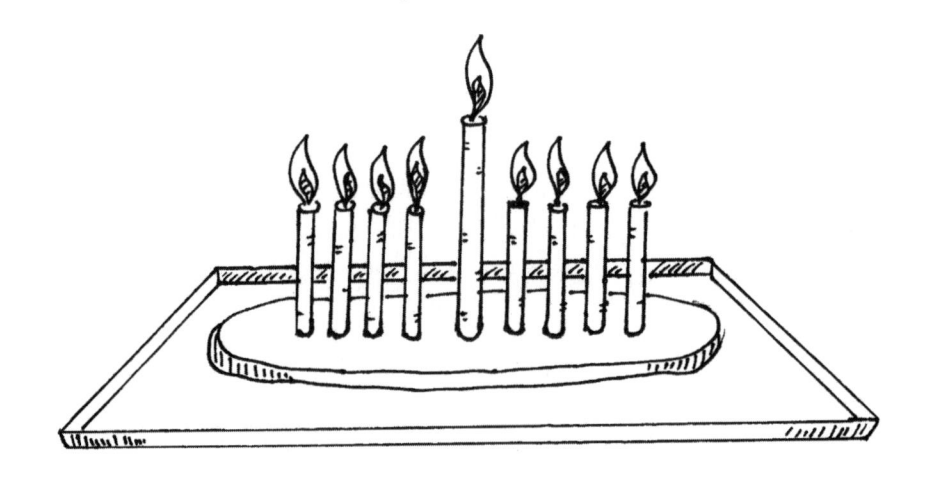

CHRISTMAS

Glitter Ball Ornaments

Stuff You Need

- solid colored glass (or plastic) ball ornaments
- tacky white glue
- gold or silver glitter
- paper clip
- paper plate or newspaper to work over

Here's a great holiday craft idea that's really super-easy. Hang 'em from your tree, use as decorations, or give one to a friend.

What You Do

Holding the ball ornament in one hand, apply the tacky white glue in swirling patterns. Work in small sections. An easy pattern to make is to draw circular lines or spirals with your glue. Just make one, then lift the glue and start a new swirl attached to the one you just finished.

Holding the ornament over the paper plate or newspaper, sprinkle a small amount of glitter over the areas where you have applied the glue. Shake off the excess onto the paper plate. (You will want to reuse this glitter!) The glitter will only stick where you have glue. You may need to gently tap the ball ornament to help shake off excess glitter.

(continued on the next page)

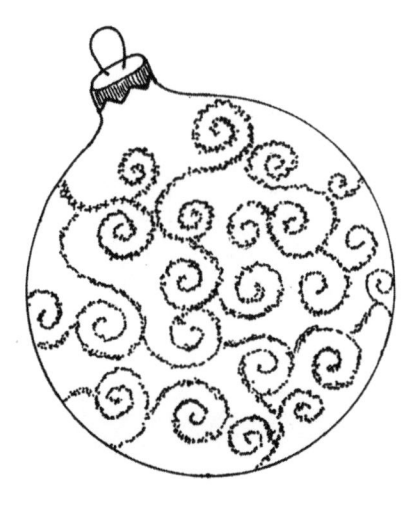

51

Glitter Ball Ornaments (cont.)

Repeat as desired until the entire ornament is decorated. Take care to hold the ornament by the top so you will prevent smudges while you are working.

Bend the paper clip into a hook shape and attach to the top of the ornament. Hang the ornament in a safe place until it is completely dry.

... Or Try This

Ornaments aren't just for decorating the tree. Add some pretty wired ribbon to the top and hang your ornament from a chandelier or light fixture, or make a series of them and hang in a window.

CHRISTMAS

Poinsettia Napkin Rings

Stuff You Need

- one small yellow pom-pom
- one 9- by 12-inch square of red felt
- one 9- by 12-inch square of green felt
- cardstock paper
- fine-line marker
- scissors
- glue
- pencil

This craft looks so special, but it comes together without a fuss. Everyone will want to know how you made it.

What You Do

Trace the patterns onto cardstock paper using a pencil. Place over your felt and draw around the patterns with a fine-line marker. You will be able to make four complete napkin rings with the two squares of 9- by 12-inch felt.

Use the patterns to cut out the felt. Remember, you will be cutting one of the green leaves and two of the red petals, plus one red ring pattern for each napkin ring.

(continued on the next page)

CUT 1 RED

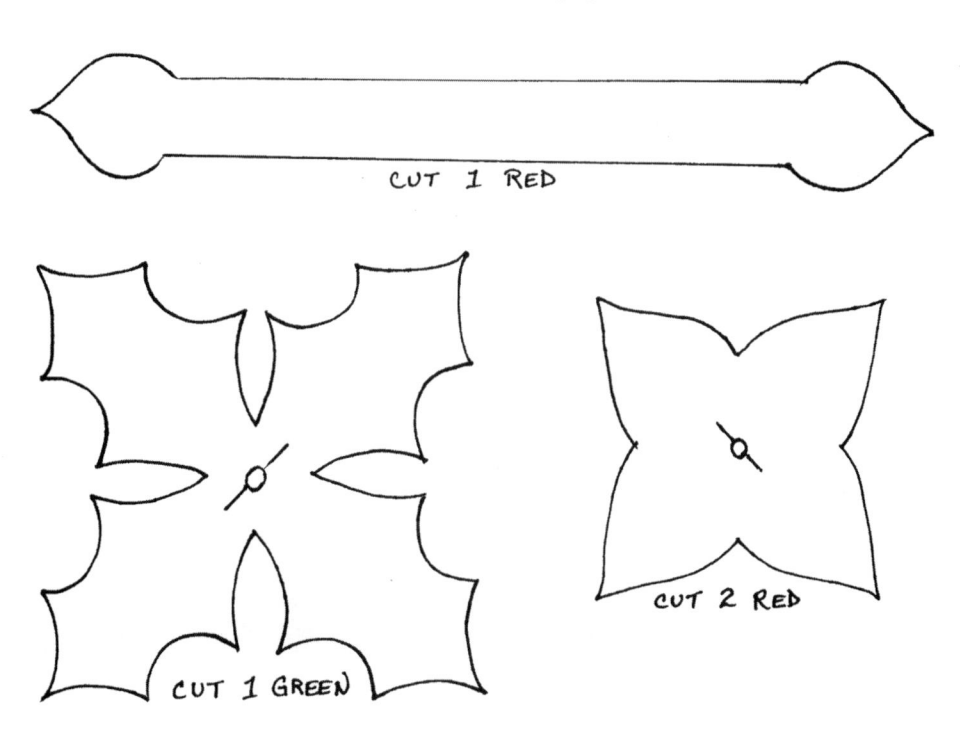

CUT 1 GREEN

CUT 2 RED

53

Poinsettia Napkin Rings (cont.)

Cut a 1/2-inch slit (as shown) in the center of your petal and leaf pieces. Make sure they are in the center so that all your pieces will fit together correctly.

Place one red petal on top of the green leaves. Rotate the next piece of red felt and lay it on top of the first, so the point of the leaves faces the opposite direction (see illustration).

Loop the ends of the long red napkin "ring" piece of felt up and through the slits, leaving the napkin "ring" loop beneath the green leaves. Fold over the last two petals (as shown).

Glue the yellow pom-pom onto the center of the flower. Let dry.

Insert your rolled napkin and set your table with style.

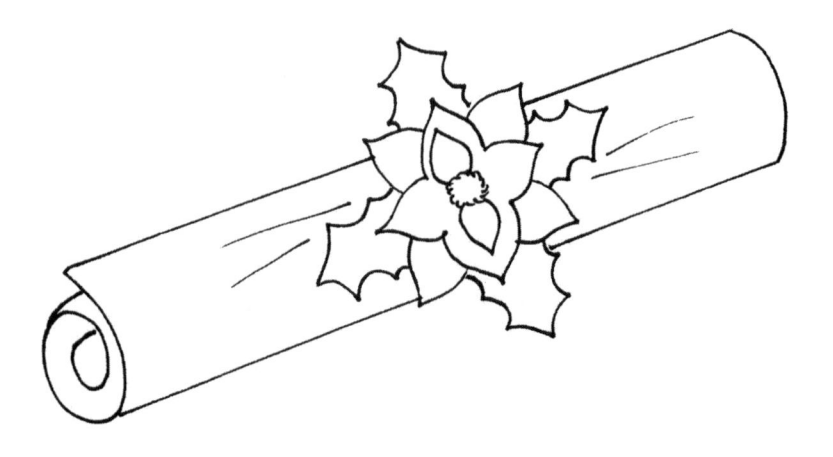

CHRISTMAS

Peppermint Stick Vase

Stuff You Need

- two dozen peppermint sticks (the large individually-wrapped ones)
- plastic cup (shorter than your peppermint sticks)
- glue (or hot glue gun with **adult supervision**)
- red ribbon
- rubber band
- marbles
- fresh flowers

Here's another super-easy gift idea. Make one for yourself and one to give to someone special!

What You Do

Unwrap the peppermint sticks and glue them around the outside of the plastic cup. Place one stick next to another until you have gone completely around. Place a rubber band around the outside to help hold them in place while you work and while they dry.

Let dry completely. Remove the rubber band.

Tie the red ribbon around the middle of the peppermint sticks.

Fill the bottom of the cup with marbles to add weight. Fill with water and arrange red and white holiday blossoms.

...Or Try This

Turn your peppermint stick container into a candy jar. When the project is completely dry, tie the red ribbon around the middle, and fill with wrapped holiday candies.

CHRISTMAS

Candy Christmas Tree

Stuff You Need

- Styrofoam cone (12-inches high with a 4-inch base works great)
- hot glue gun and glue sticks
- two pounds of assorted hard candies in holiday colors (try ribbon candy, mints, and jellybeans)
- **Note:** Tacky glue (at craft stores) may be substituted for the hot glue or add one part cornstarch to three parts glue to thicken white craft glue

Adult supervision required

Here's a holiday craft that looks good enough to eat, but it's just for feasting your eyes on!

What You Do

Starting with the largest candy pieces, glue them about 2-inches apart all around the cone.

Fill in by gluing the medium-sized candy pieces in empty spaces.

Finish by gluing the small candies and jellybeans down, until none of the Styrofoam cone shows.

...Or Try This

For an extra-special touch, place your decorated candy tree on a paper doily, which will give it a nice "tree skirt" effect!

Careful! Ask an adult to help you use the hot glue gun.

Beaded Wreath Pin

Stuff You Need

- one pipe cleaner (red or green)
- 11 red and 33 green tri-beads (available at bead stores)
- pin-backing
- glue
- scissors
- 9-inch long gold ribbon (1/4- by 1/2-inch wide)

Wear this adorable wreath to signal the beginning of the holiday season or to give as an awesome gift.

What You Do

Make a small, loose loop in one end of the pipe cleaner. This will prevent the beads from falling off while threading. Tri-beads are designed to fit together which you will discover as you thread them.

Thread beads onto the pipe cleaner: three green ones, followed by one red. Repeat until the pipe cleaner has 3 inches left on either end. Unbend the loop.

Form the pipe cleaner into a circle, leaving the un-beaded ends free. Twist the pipe cleaner ends together securely and snip off the excess with the scissors.

Tie the gold ribbon around the twisted ends in a pretty bow.

Glue the pin-back onto the back of the wreath.

CHRISTMAS

Wreath of Hands

Stuff You Need

- green and red construction paper
- scissors
- pencil
- glue
- green marker (or green paint and a paintbrush)
- red tissue paper
- paper plate

This is a great craft to do with a friend. You'll discover lots of different, creative ways to use your "hands" — like for gift tags, as tree garlands or as a decorative border around your windows.

What You Do

Using a pencil, trace your hand onto the green construction paper. Cut out. Repeat approximately twelve times for the wreath. Friends or family members can add their hands to it!

Cut a circle about 2 inches in diameter out of the inside of a paper plate, leaving a hole in the middle. Color around the outside with the green marker or paint green. Let dry.

(continued on the next page)

Wreath of Hands (cont.)

Glue hand "leaves" around the circle, overlapping each a little.

Cut the red tissue paper into 2-inch squares. Crumple and roll the tissue paper into little "berries." Glue these onto the wreath.

Draw and cut a bow out of red construction paper. Glue this to the bottom of the wreath.

... Or Try This

Place your hand in clay and trace around it. Cut it out with a plastic knife. Use a straw to drill a hole in it while still damp. Using a toothpick, write your name and the date — and each year you can hang a new one from your tree!

CHRISTMAS

Candy Cane Reindeer

Stuff You Need

- one (wrapped) large curved candy cane
- two brown pipe cleaners
- thin green ribbon
- two "wiggly eyes" (from craft store)
- one small red pom-pom
- scissors
- glue

This project is fun to make with a group of friends! Use your reindeer as ornaments for your tree, stocking stuffers, or attached to your gift wrap for an extra-special touch.

What You Do

Twist one long pipe cleaner around the candy cane at the bend, letting the two ends stick up at the top. Cut the other pipe cleaner in half. Twist a short pipe cleaner around both of the long pipe cleaner ends to create the antlers.

Glue on the "wiggly eyes" and nose. **Note:** If you can't find the "wiggly eyes" in a craft store, substitute black felt cut into small circles.

Tie the green ribbon around the "neck" of the candy cane.

CHRISTMAS

Pinecone Christmas Tree

Stuff You Need

- one pinecone
- red and green acrylic paint
- paintbrush
- paper plate
- glitter
- cranberries (or red tissue paper)
- jar lid
- nail
- hammer
- ribbon
- glue
- newspaper to cover work area

Adult supervision required

Here's a nature craft that will brighten up any Christmas. Great as a gift, too!

What You Do

Pour a small amount of red paint onto a paper plate. Paint the jar lid red. Let dry.

Hammer nail into the top of the jar lid, with the nail facing up when the lid is facing top-side down (as shown).

Put a bit of glue onto the nail and work the pinecone onto it. (**Note:** If the cone is difficult to attach to the nail, ask an adult to drill a tiny hole in the bottom of the pinecone.)

Pour a small amount of green paint onto a paper plate. Use the brush and paint the entire cone. While the paint is still wet, sprinkle on lots of glitter.

When dry, glue on cranberries, or make some out of tiny red tissue paper balls (cut 1-inch squares of tissue paper and crumple and roll into ball shapes).

Careful! Ask an adult to help you use the hammer.

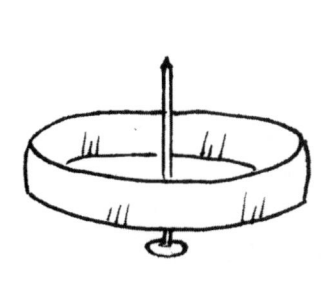

61

Cinnamon Stick Candle

Stuff You Need

- 3-inch pillar candle in white or a holiday color
- cinnamon sticks (approximately 24)
- 36-inch lengths of raffia
- tacky glue
- ice cream stick or plastic knife
- rubber band
- waxed paper to cover work area

This project makes a beautiful craft. Use a plain or scented candle and wrap it up in sweet-smelling cinnamon sticks.

What You Do

Working in small sections, pour some tacky glue onto the surface of the candle. (Note: If you can't find tacky glue at a craft store, you can thicken white craft glue by using one part cornstarch to three parts glue.) Use the ice cream stick or plastic knife to smear the glue evenly from the bottom edge almost up to the top of the candle.

Press cinnamon sticks evenly around the sides, pressing them into the glue as you work.

Repeat this process until the entire candle is covered.

Hold in place with the rubber band. Let dry completely on the waxed paper.

Tie several 36-inch lengths of raffia around the middle of the candle and make a bow. Red or green looks nice for Christmas, blue for Hanukkah. Trim the ends, if needed.

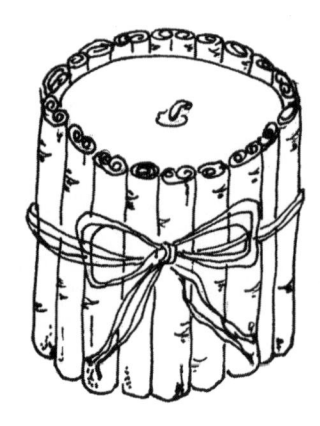

CHRISTMAS

Clay Ornaments

Stuff You Need

- homemade clay (see recipe)
- paint — acrylic, craft, or tempera
- paintbrush
- ribbon
- straw
- cookie cutters
- rolling pin
- wax paper to cover your work surface

Adult supervision required

Make this a special holiday with handmade ornaments to decorate your home!

What You Do

Make the clay by mixing in a large bowl:

- 2 cups flour
- 1/2 cup salt
- 1/2 cup water
- 1 tablespoon cooking oil

Knead five minutes. Roll out dough to 1/4 inch thickness.

Use cookie cutters to cut out the designs.

Twirl a straw through the top to drill a hole for hanging.

Place on a cookie sheet and bake one hour at 350 degrees. Carefully remove from oven and let cool.

Use paint to decorate. Add ribbon to hang.

Careful! Ask an adult to help you when using the oven and handling the hot cookie sheet.

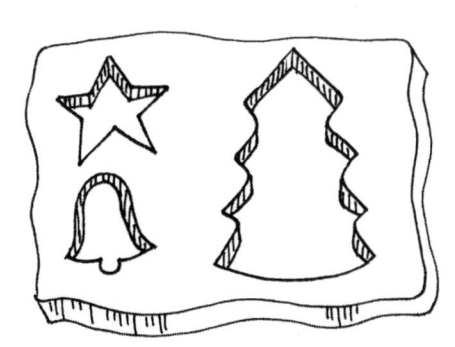

Punched-Tin Candle Holder

Stuff You Need

- one empty tin can
- hammer and nail
- marker
- small votive candle
- ruler
- scissors
- paper
- tape
- towel or rag
- optional: acrylic paint

Adult supervision required

What You Do

Ask an adult to help you remove the top of a can. Remove wrapper, being sure to remove all paper residue. Fill the can with water and place in the freezer.

Remove from freezer when water is frozen solid (several hours).

Measure and cut a piece of paper to fit around the outside of the can. Use the marker to draw a pattern. Think of holiday motifs such as stars, bells, wreaths, or trees.

Wrap the paper around the can and tape the edges together. Place the can on its side and place a towel under it to catch any drips as the ice melts. Punch holes with the hammer and nail around the lines of the design.

Remove paper and any remaining ice. Dry the can. Paint if desired.

Place votive candle in bottom of can.

Careful! Ask for an adult's help when using the hammer and lighting the candle.

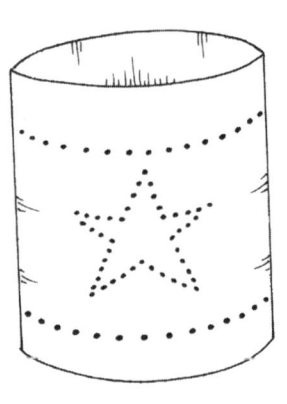

CHRISTMAS

Gold Pasta Wreath

Stuff You Need

- paper plate
- gold acrylic paint
- paintbrush
- assorted shapes of pasta
- gold glitter glue
- gold or silver beads
- pencil
- small piece of wire for hanging
- hole punch
- scissors
- newspaper to cover work area

It's amazing how gold paint can turn ordinary pasta into a unique decoration.

What You Do

Draw a circle in the middle of the paper plate. You can use a plate, bowl, or other round shape to help. Draw around it as your guide, then cut out the center, making sure you leave a solid paper ring at least 2 inches wide.

Punch two holes about an inch apart, side by side, and about 1 inch down from the top of the paper plate. Loop the small piece of wire through the loops and wrap ends together to make a hanger.

(continued on the next page)

Gold Pasta Wreath (cont.)

Working in sections, apply white craft glue to one area. Add pasta on top of the glue. Use large sections to apply the first layer, then add more glue and pasta to build up additional layers. Let dry overnight.

Paint the entire surface with the gold paint and sprinkle on gold glitter while the paint is still wet.

If desired, add "ornaments" of gold and silver costume jewelry beads.

... Or Try This

You can use this technique to make a tree by using a plastic foam cone as your base, then following the directions above. Place a pretty gold or silver paper doily under the tree.

Beaded Fruit

Stuff You Need

- artificial fruit such as apples, pears, or bananas (found in craft or fabric stores)
- tacky glue
- 6mm round glass beads in colors to match fruit
- green construction paper
- pencil
- scissors
- wax paper to cover work area

Here's a super-easy way to imitate the age-old craft of beading and create a gift your mom, aunt, grandmother, or teacher (think apples) will love.

What You Do

The secret to this craft is to work in small areas. Brush on a small amount of the "tacky" white craft glue to a one-inch section. (Note: If you can't find tacky glue at a craft store, use cornstarch to thicken white craft glue. You'll need one part cornstarch to three parts glue.)

Press the glass beads into the glue. Hold in place with some pressure to let the glue "set" before beginning on a new section.

Repeat until the entire fruit is covered. Let dry on the wax paper.

Draw a small leaf shape on the green construction paper. Cut out and glue to the top of the fruit.

. . . Or Try This

Several of these arranged in a glass bowl will shine brightly and will reflect any shimmering holiday lights you may have nearby!

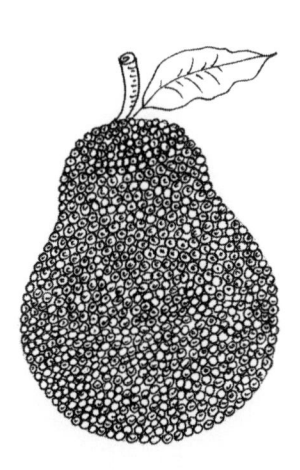

CHRISTMAS

Paper Cone Ornament

Stuff You Need

- colored construction paper
- pencil
- crayons or markers
- 1/2 yard of narrow ribbon
- 1/2 yard of lace
- glue
- stapler
- scissors
- candy

Fill this ornament with candies and hang on the tree, or make several and give them as gifts!

What You Do

Using your construction paper, draw and cut out a half circle with a 10 1/2-inch diameter. You can use a bowl, a plate or any other round shape that's the right size as a guide. Color with the markers or crayons as desired.

To form a cone, find the half-way point of the straight edge. Bring the two edges together, overlapping about an inch at the top to form your cone-like shape. Keep your point at the bottom. Glue together. Hold the seams until set (or secure with a staple at top).

Glue lace around the inside top edge so lace sticks up all around.

(continued on the next page)

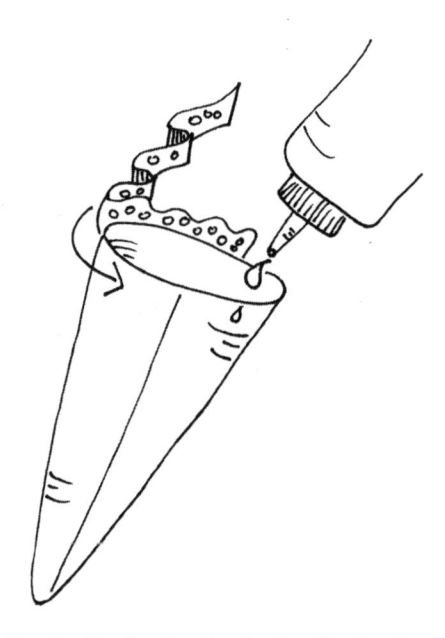

CHRISTMAS

Paper Cone Ornament (cont.)

Glue the ribbon around the outside top edge. Cut an 8-inch piece of ribbon and add to the top as a handle. Glue or staple.

Fill with gumdrops or other holiday candy and enjoy!

. . . Or Try This

Use a sugar cone (ice cream cone). Find a "Royal Icing" recipe in a holiday cookbook and decorate with icing designs, such as swirls, dots, and lines, and "glue" on candy decorations using extra icing. Gently poke two holes about 1/2" down from the top on opposite sides and tie a ribbon for a handle. Fill with more candies!

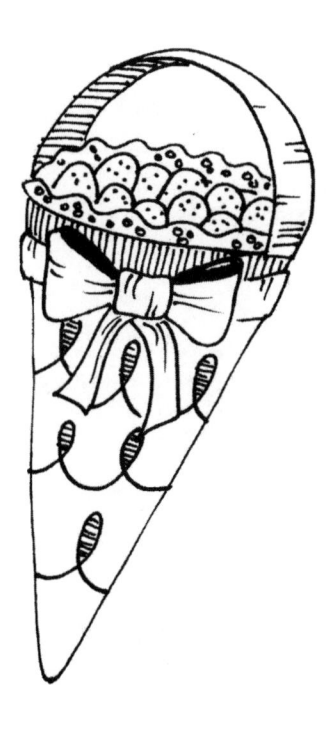

CHRISTMAS

Tissue Paper Trees

Stuff You Need

- corrugated cardboard (old box)
- scissors
- pencil
- glue
- one package of green and several sheets of red tissue paper
- green paint
- paintbrush — acrylic, craft, or tempera
- glitter (optional)

These trees make a great centerpiece for a holiday table.

What You Do

Draw a pattern for a Christmas tree with a flat bottom, about 6 to 8 inches tall. Trace and cut out two of these from the corrugated cardboard.

Paint the tree pieces green. Let dry.

Using scissors, have an adult help you make a slit from the top of one tree, down the center, about halfway the length of the tree. Make another slit from the bottom of the other tree, up from the center, about halfway the length of the tree.

(continued on the next page)

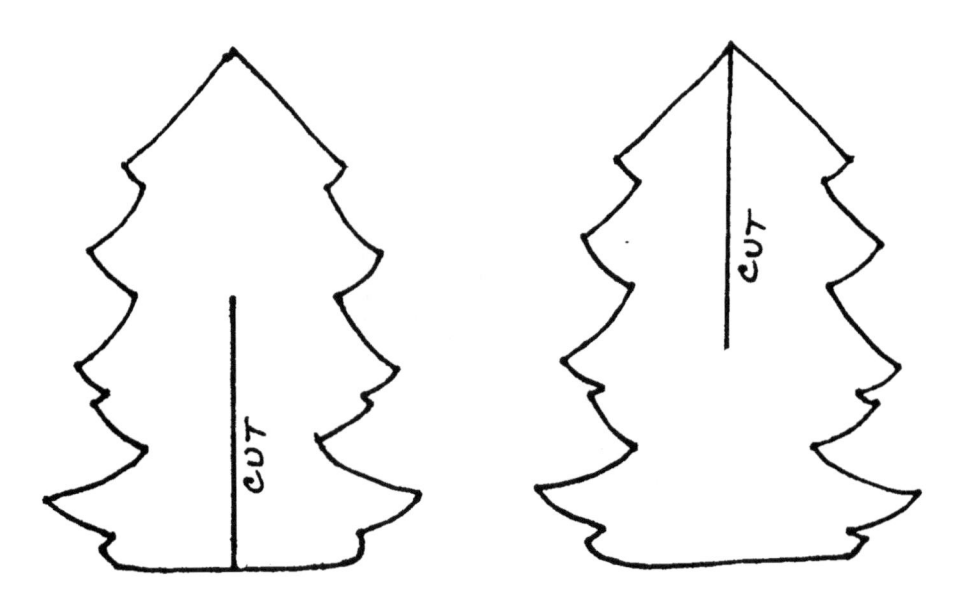

Tissue Paper Trees

Fit the trees together by inserting the bottom slit into top slit. They will now stand up!

Cut green tissue paper into lots of (several hundred) 1-inch squares. Wrap each piece of tissue paper around the flat-eraser end of a pencil, forming fanned-out leaves. Dip into a small amount of white glue and press onto the tree. Repeat until all surfaces are filled with the green tissue.

Cut red tissue paper into 2-inch squares. Crumple each square into a small ball. Glue onto the tree wherever you wish to add a decoration. If desired, place a dab of glue onto the top side of the balls and sprinkle on some glitter to add sparkle to your trees.

Kwanzaa Woven Placemat

Stuff You Need

- red, green, and black construction paper
- scissors
- ruler
- glue

Help make your holiday table look festive as your family celebrates this special holiday!

What You Do

Select one color of the construction paper to serve as your "background" color. Fold this paper in half with the short sides together.

Use your ruler to draw a line one inch from the outer edge of the paper, opposite the folded side, down the length of the short side. This is your "stop" line, meaning you will never cut through or past this line.

Turn your ruler sideways and draw lines spaced evenly one-inch apart, horizontally, going from the "stop" line to the folded edge.

(continued on the next page)

Kwanzaa Woven Placemat (cont.)

Beginning at the folded edge, cut the lines, remembering to stop at the "stop" line.

Cut 1-inch strips from the other two colors of construction paper.

Unfold your background paper and begin weaving one of the 1-inch cut pieces of paper by sliding it over and under your background paper. Slide the first woven strip as close to the "stop" line as possible when finished. Add a drop of glue to the under side of the ends to keep them in place.

Repeat with the next 1-inch cut strip of paper. Use another color and weave in an opposite manner. This means if you started the last strip over, then this strip will start under the background paper. Repeat with remaining strips until the background paper is fully woven.

If desired, use the scissors to create a fringe on the ends of the woven paper.

Repeat for as many placemats as needed.

Beaded Candles

Stuff You Need

- a square white candle (a 4-inch pillar works great)
- straight pins
- red and green seed beads
- black sequins

Adult supervision required

Here's a way to make a beautiful centerpiece or decoration for Kwanzaa!

What You Do

You can do this craft several ways. One idea is to create a specific design on your candle. Something simple like a star or heart works great. The other is to create an abstract design without a specific pattern. The technique will be the same for both.

Thread a red or green seed bead, followed by a sequin onto a straight pin.

(continued on the next page)

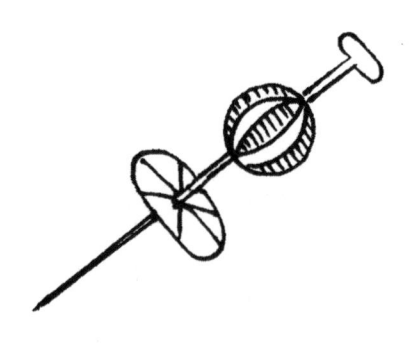

Beaded Candles (cont.)

Stick the beaded straight pins into the candle, either randomly for your abstract design, or following a pattern.

Repeat until you are pleased with the design you have created. Try making several candles using the red, green, and black colors of Kwanzaa, alternating the colors for each.

...Or Try This

You can also make this craft using colored or silver and gold rhinestones. Glue them onto your candle for an extra-special candle that adds sparkle to your holiday!

Careful! Always ask an adult to help you light the candles.

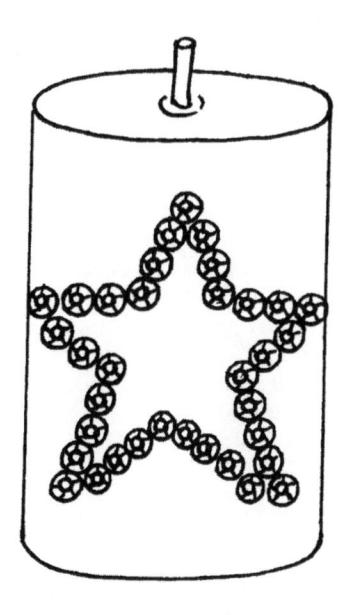

New Year's Eve Party Hat

Stuff You Need

- poster board
- markers
- stapler
- construction paper
- tape measure
- scissors
- glue
- one package of 1/4-inch elastic
- pom-pom

Celebrate the New Year with style in this fun party hat!

What You Do

Measure the circumference of your head, then add one inch. To make the cone for the hat, draw a half-circle onto the poster board (with a flat, straight bottom) with a curve the length of this circumference measurement (see illustration). Use a plate, bowl, or other round shape in the correct size. Draw around it as your guide. Cut it out from your poster board.

Decorate as desired with markers.

(continued on the next page)

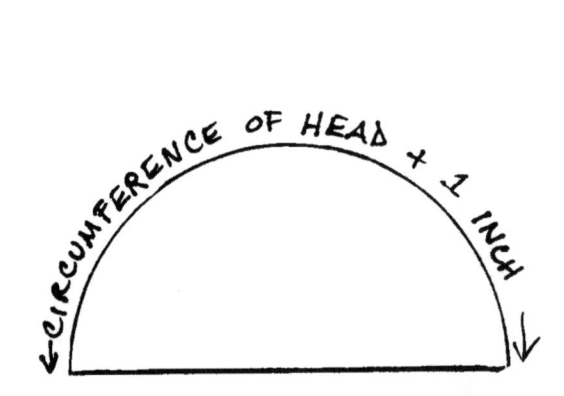

New Year's Eve Party Hat (cont.)

To form the cone, find the half-way point of the straight edge. Bring the two edges up together and overlap till your shape is cone-like. Then staple or glue seams shut.

Measure and cut elastic to fit from ear to ear, under your chin. Staple elastic to sides to form chinstrap.

Cut a 3-inch strip of construction paper to the length of head circumference. Cut 1-inch fringe down on the top and bottom of your paper. Wrap fringe around a pencil to curl. Glue around bottom of hat.

Glue pom-pom on top of hat.

... Or Try This

Add a long scarf instead of a pom-pom and make princess hats.

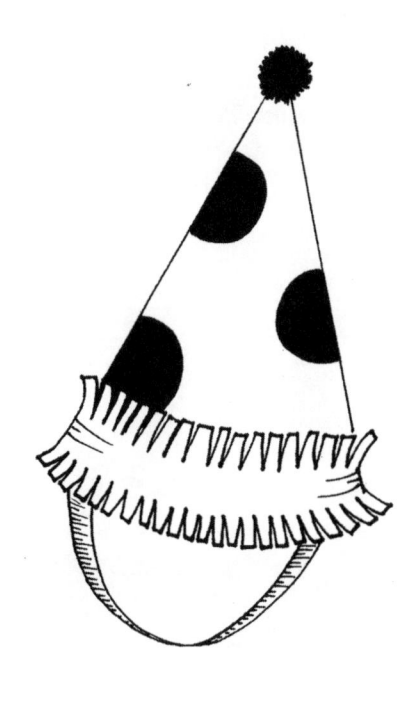

NEW YEAR'S EVE

New Year Confetti Placemats

Stuff You Need

- 12- by 18-inch construction paper
- old toothbrush
- brightly colored paints — acrylic, craft, or tempera
- rubber gloves
- scissors
- gold and silver stick-on stars
- clear contact paper
- small paper cups for paint (one for each color)
- newspaper to cover work area

Let the party begin. Bring in the New Year with style with these cool handmade placemats!

What You Do

Pour the paint in the paper cups. Use a different cup for each color paint.

Put on the rubber gloves. An apron or old T-shirt is a good idea for this craft because part of its fun is that it's messy!

Dip the toothbrush in one color of the paint. Point the brush down so the bristles are facing towards the paper. Run your thumb or finger across the bristles so the paint is sprayed and splattered onto the paper. Repeat all around the paper, and with different colors until you have a design you like. Let dry.

Add the star stickers.

Cut two pieces of clear contact paper slightly larger than the placemat. Peel off the backing paper and seal to both sides of placemat, smoothing out any air bubbles.

Repeat for as many placemats as needed.

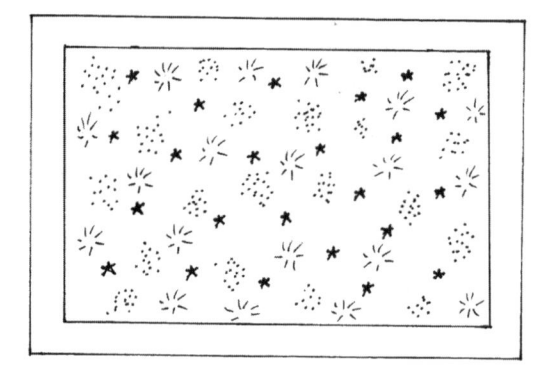

New Year's Eve Party Favors

Stuff You Need

- empty toilet paper tube (one tube makes two favors)
- tissue paper in holiday colors
- scissors
- confetti (purchased or make your own)
- glue stick
- ribbon

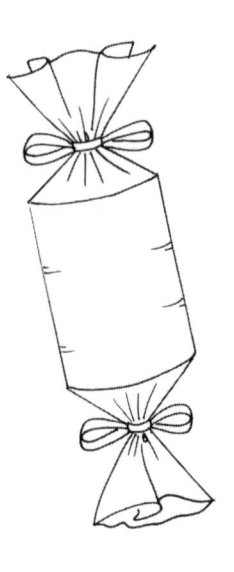

Everyone loves those famous Poppers. Here's a way you can make your own party favors for one of the best nights of the year!

What You Do

Cut toilet paper tube in half making two cylinders. Cut the tissue paper into 18- by 12-inch sheets for each party favor.

Center the toilet paper tube at the edge of the 12-inch side of tissue paper and begin rolling the tissue around it. Make sure your tube is centered before you do your rolling. The tissue should cover it completely about three times. Glue the seams closed.

Cut your ribbon into 6-inch lengths and gather the tissue paper at one end of the party favor. Tie a bow with the ribbon.

Fill with confetti. If you don't want to purchase confetti you can make your own by combining glitter and tiny pieces of cut paper.

Gather the other end of the tissue paper and tie a bow with another 6-inch piece of ribbon.

During your party you can untie one end, and release your confetti!

... Or Try This

Another fun idea is to use this technique as a unique gift wrapper. You can fit many small items inside, or use a larger paper towel roll for the tube and place larger items inside. You can also fill with candies or other treats and give at the end of a party as favors!

Treasure Box

Stuff You Need

- small white jewelry-style gift box with lid
- glue
- glitter
- sequins, beads, rhinestone jewels, foil stars, or other decorations
- scissors
- white paper
- pen
- ribbon or string
- newspaper to cover work area

This is a fun little box to decorate and use to store all of your New Year's resolutions. You can take them out during the year and see how you are doing!

What You Do

Put glue all over the lid of the box. Sprinkle on glitter.

Add sequins, rhinestones, old jewelry, beads, and any other desired decorations. Set aside to dry.

Repeat to sides of box, if desired. Allow time for each side of the box to dry so everything can "set" before beginning work on a new side.

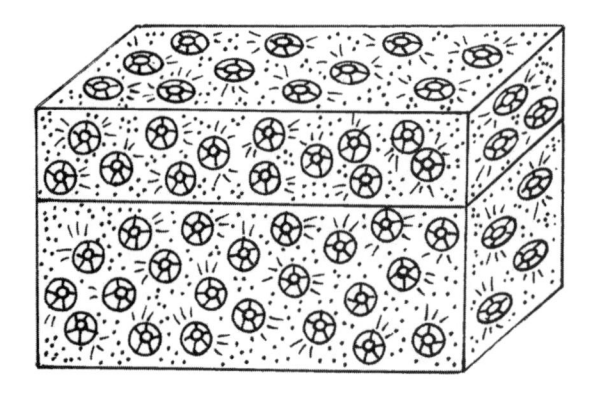

(continued on the next page)

Treasure Box (cont.)

Make tiny "Resolution Scrolls" to put inside your box. Cut your white paper to the size of a 2- by 3-inch card. Write a different resolution on each piece of paper or record a goal you have for the coming year. Roll up each piece of paper and tie with a piece of ribbon or string. Place your little scrolls in your treasure box.

... Or Try This

Make a memorable party invitation by decorating a box for each guest and filling it with a handmade invitation scroll. You can also make Treasure Boxes to store any of your tiny trinkets or to give as party favors.

Make Your Own Clay

Adult Supervision Required

Stuff You Need

- 2 cups flour
- 1/2 cup salt
- 1/2 cup water
- 1 tablespoon vegetable oil

Recipe #1

Knead five minutes.

After shaping into your craft, bake in 350-degree oven for one hour.

Unused clay will keep in refrigerator for two weeks.

Store in a sealed, air-tight plastic bag.

Stuff You Need

- 1/2 cup cornstarch
- 1/3 cup water
- 1 cup salt
- 1/3 cup water

Recipe #2

In one bowl dissolve cornstarch in 1/2 cup water.

In pan mix salt and 1/3 cup water.

Heat and stir until it boils.

Remove from heat and mix both together.

This dough will be thick. Knead until smooth.

Keep sealed in plastic bag for up to two weeks.

Can be air-dried or baked after shaping into your craft. If baking, use a 200-degree oven for one hour.

Stuff You Need

- 1 1/2 cup flour
- 1/2 cup salt
- 1/4 cup vegetable oil
- 1/2 cup water

Recipe #3

Mix and knead 3-5 minutes.

Store in sealed container for up to two weeks.

Can be air-dried or baked after shaping into your craft. If baking, use 325-degree oven for one hour.

Careful! Ask for an adult's help when using the stove or oven.

Acknowledgments

Thanks so much to Roxanne Camron, without whom this project would not have come together, and thank you also to Kelly, Emma, and the students of Westlake Elementary for their creative spirits, and to Joy Talley for her inspiration.

About the Author

Nancy Jo King has been a professional artist and teacher for more than 15 years. Her work has been featured in exhibits nationwide, including the National Association of Art Educators' annual convention. She has a passion for children's arts, and has been a craft designer for young adult magazines such as *Smackers* and *All About You*. King taught at the elementary level for many years, and has written, developed, and facilitated a curriculum for K-6 visual arts education. She lives in Southern California with her son and daughter.